Bugs Bunny's Favorite Jokes

ILLUSTRATED BY ANIMATED ARTS

A GOLDEN BOOK · NEW YORK

WESTERN PUBLISHING COMPANY, INC., RACINE, WISCONSIN 53404

Bugs: Daffy, you remind me of being on the ocean.

Daffy: Do you mean I'm romantic and wild?

Bugs: No, you just make me sick!

Elmer: Every time I pass a pretty girl, she sighs.
Bugs: Yeah . . . with relief!

Yosemite Sam: There's one thing a-preyin' on my mind.

Bugs: Don't worry. It'll soon die of starvation.

Daffy: I didn't come here to be insulted.
Bugs: Where do you usually go?

Bugs: I won an award at summer camp for saving everybody's life!

Porky: Th-th-that's wonderful! How did you do it?

Bugs: I got rid of the cook.

Miss Prissy: Whatever did you do when the ship sank in the middle of the ocean?

Foghorn Leghorn: Ma'am, I just grabbed a bar of soap and washed myself ashore.

Elmer: How long can a person live without a brain?

Bugs: I give up. How old are you?

Daffy: Whenever I get up onstage, people clap their hands!

Bugs: Yeah . . . over their eyes!

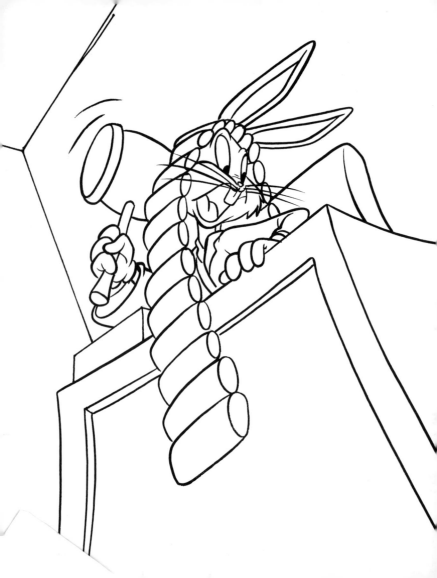

Judge: Since the jury has found you not guilty of robbing the bank, you are free to go.

Yosemite Sam: Does that mean I can keep the money?

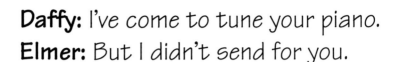

Daffy: I've come to tune your piano.
Elmer: But I didn't send for you.
Daffy: I know, but your
neighbors did.

What did Bugs give to the vampire
for his cold?
Coffin syrup.

Sylvester: How did you do on your first day of school?

Sylvester Jr.: Not so well, I guess. I have to go back tomorrow.

Bugs: Is your new horse well behaved?

Yosemite Sam: Yup! Whenever we get to a fence, he stops and lets me go over first.

Witch Hazel: I'm as gruesome as ever!

Bugs: Yup! After all these years, you've managed to keep your ghoulish figure!

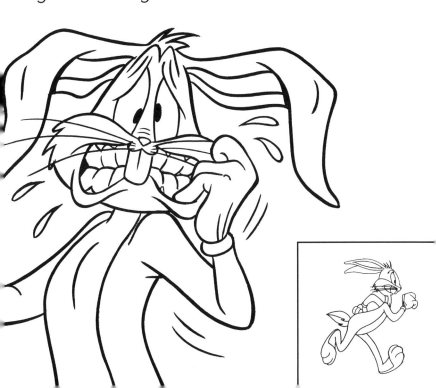

What do you get when you throw
Daffy Duck in the Atlantic Ocean?
Saltwater Daffy.

Elmer: Don't I sing wike a bird?
Bugs: Yeah . . . and you've got the brain to match!

Sylvester Jr.: Father, Father, I caught a green parakeet. Can I eat him?
Sylvester: Of course not! Let him go, then try to catch a ripe one.

Bugs: Did you hear that Yosemite Sam brushed his teeth with gun powder by mistake?

Daffy: What happened?

Bugs: He spent the rest of the day shooting off his mouth.

What does Wile E. Coyote say when someone wants to know why he has never caught the Road Runner?

"Don't ACME that!"

Daffy: I have a mind of my own.
Bugs: Of course. Nobody else wants it.

Porky Pig: I've come to ask for your hand in m-m-marriage.

Petunia Pig: I'm sorry, but you'll have to take all of me.

Judge: Why did you hit the clock?
Yosemite Sam: It was self-defense! The clock struck first!

JURY

Elmer: Is it okay if I eat dinner at your place tonight?

Bugs: Do you mind eating last week's leftovers?

Elmer: No.

Bugs: Good. Then come over next week.

Daffy: The doctor told me to drink some grape juice after a hot bath.
Porky: How was the g-g-grape juice?
Daffy: I don't know. I'm still drinking the hot bath.

Yosemite Sam: Let me tell you about myself, varmint.
Bugs: Good, I enjoy horror stories.

Henery Hawk: I'm standing tall, chicken!

Foghorn Leghorn: Tall? Son, you're so short, you ask babies for piggyback rides.

Daffy: I'm known for my exciting personality.

Bugs: Exciting personality? You're so boring, if you threw a boomerang, it wouldn't come back to you.

Taz's Mom: Taz, what are you doing with that duck?

Taz: Chasing him 'round tree.

Taz's Mom: How many times have I told you not to play with your food?

Porky: Do you know how many sheep it takes to make one sweater?
Daffy: I didn't even know they could knit!

Yosemite Sam: I have the face of a saint.

Bugs: You sure do—a Saint Bernard.

Sylvester: I'm going to catch you this time!

Speedy Gonzales: You're so slow, you couldn't catch a cold!

Elmer: I'm not myself today.
Bugs: I noticed the improvement immediately.

Yosemite Sam: I heard your cat drowned in a barrel of varnish. It must have been an awful way to go.

Granny: No, actually he had a beautiful finish!

Taz: You think Taz cute?

Bugs: Cute? You're so scary-looking, an echo would be afraid to answer you!

Ham Sandwich: *Give me a double malted milkshake.*

Daffy: *Sorry, we don't serve food here.*

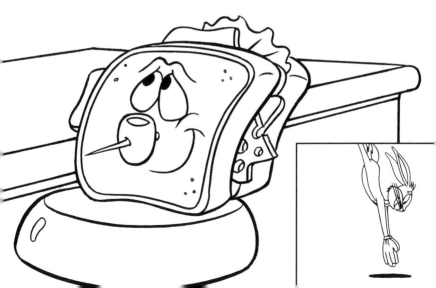

Elmer: I'm a vewy quiet guy.
Bugs: Wrong! Your mouth is so big,
you can sing a duet by yourself.

Foghorn Leghorn: My cousin, ah-say cousin, is a famous lion tamer. His special trick is putting his right hand in the lion's mouth.

Miss Prissy: Oh, my! What's your cousin's name?

Foghorn Leghorn: Lefty.

Daffy: I have the face of a movie star.

Bugs: Well, you better give it back. You're messing it up.

Sylvester: I've changed my mind.
Speedy Gonzales: Great, señor! I hope the new one works better.

Yosemite Sam: Varmint, do you think I'm tall enough to play basketball?

Bugs: You kiddin'? You're so short, you wear socks to keep your neck warm.

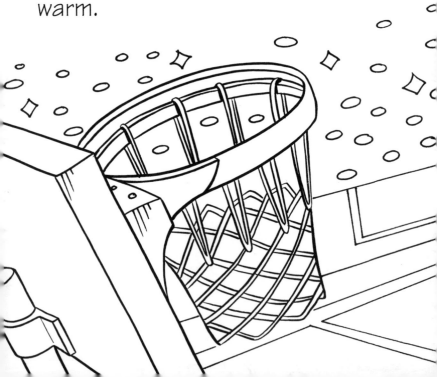

Elmer: That picture doesn't do me justice.

Bugs: With a face like that, you don't need justice—you need mercy.

What did Porky Pig say to Petunia
about her scrambled eggs?
"Th-th-that's all yokes!"